TERROR

ON

TULIP

LANE

ANNE SCHRAFF

STANDING TALL MYSTERIES
BY ANNE SCHRAFF

Project Editor: Carol E. Newell
Cover Designer and Illustrator: TSA design group

© 1995 Saddleback Publishing, Inc.

SADDLEBACK
PUBLISHING • INC.

3505 Cadillac Ave., Building F-9
Costa Mesa, CA 92626

ISBN 1-56254-157-9
Printed in the United States of America
03 02 01 M 99 98 97 96 8 7 6 5 4 3 2 1

Chapter 1

Hakeem Kemp caught the bus across town to his new job at 8 Tulip Lane. He and his family lived in an apartment in a working class neighborhood of Cambodian restaurants, Ethiopian delis, and African American art galleries. Hakeem's parents made beautiful lamps and mirrors.

It was a far cry from Hakeem's street to the elegance of Tulip Lane. A single house sold for as much money as a block of houses where Hakeem lived. It seemed like a dream job at first—babysitting ten year old Maurice Nash, the son of basketball superstar Dale Nash.

"We want a young man to be with

our son from 2:30 to 7:00 each day," Nash explained. "I never know when I'm home and my wife's business takes most of the day. Maurice is interested in science, and you're an honors student in science at your high school, Hakeem. So you two should get along just fine."

Hakeem couldn't believe his good fortune in getting such a job—until he met the *real* Maurice Nash.

"Hi, Hakeem," Maurice had smiled politely that first day in the presence of his parents. "Hey, that's a cool name."

Maurice's parents beamed. "Maurice is an outstanding student. He's always winning in the Science Fair. He's gifted, very gifted," Dale Nash had said.

"He'll be no trouble at all, Hakeem," Jessa Nash said. "Just help him with his more difficult homework and be a companion. Most of the time he'll be working on his computer anyway, and you won't even know he's in the house."

Hakeem had been thrilled. He desperately needed money for college. Next fall he was starting his senior year in high school. He had only been able to get a job delivering pizzas. This job with the Nash family paid well. And Hakeem was a real fan of Dale Nash on the basketball court. He had some of the flair that made Michael Jordan great.

But yesterday, Hakeem's first day, Maurice showed his true colors. Hakeem was there early. He raced over from school so he could greet Maurice as he came home.

"Hi, Maurice," Hakeem had said. "I put out your snack. Your Mom said you like granola bars and chocolate milk."

Maurice tossed his books on the couch, missing the target. Two of them fell to the floor. "Go pick 'em up, Hakeem," he said, flopping down in a leather recliner.

Hakeem was shocked by the boy's rudeness. He picked up the books and said, "Those are peanut butter granola bars. Your mother said …"

"What does she know? She's never here. I hate granola bars. Go to the fridge and get me some chocolate bars and root beer," Maurice said. "Double time!"

Hakeem stared at the boy. "But your parents said …"

"You're working for me now, Hakeem. If you don't suit me you're outta here, got it? Now get busy," Maurice snapped his fingers.

"Chocolate bars and root beer aren't nutritious for a growing boy," Hakeem said.

"Hakeem, listen up. You're my servant. My gopher. So go for my goodies or when Mom comes home tonight I'll tell them to can you. It all depends on me if you stay or go," Maurice said.

Now, on his second day, Hakeem

dreaded the boy's return from school. He went to Tulip Lane as usual and put out the raisin muffins and chocolate milk Mrs. Nash had ordered.

Maurice came home. He took one look at the muffins and hurled them against the wall. They exploded, spraying raisins all over the rug. "Uh-oh, a cleaning job for you, Hakeem. But first, get me some candy and ice cream."

"Maurice, I promised your parents I'd give you what they asked," Hakeem said. Maurice sneered and looked Hakeem right in the eye. "You want to be fired, man?" he demanded.

Chapter 2

Hakeem brought the boy what he wanted and then cleaned up the remnants of the muffins. Hakeem felt used and bitter, but he kept reminding himself how good the money was. He was earning more here in a week than he could earn delivering pizzas in a month.

Maurice reclined in his chair watching Hakeem sweep up crumbs. "You're poor, aren't you? I can tell. Poor people have run down shoes and cheap clothes. You really got cheap clothes. I bet you buy 'em at the thrift stores," Maurice said.

"My family isn't rich but they work hard," Hakeem said.

"Mom and Pop say we gotta be nice to poor people," Maurice said, "but I think poor people are boring. We've always been rich. Pop makes megabucks."

Hakeem clenched his teeth.

"Is everybody poor in your neighborhood? I bet you live in a crummy apartment, huh, with a bunch of brothers and sisters." Maurice finished his ice cream. "I gotta write a book report on the rain forest. It's a boring topic. Dad said you do okay in school, but you're not gifted like me. But I guess it'd be okay to let you do my book report on the rain forest while I watch TV."

"You'd better do your own book report," Hakeem said.

"Dad said you'd help me with my homework. You'd better, Hakeem. I've had four babysitters. They all got fired because I wanted them fired. Get the picture? I could do the book report easy—because I'm a genius—but it's boring, so you'll do it." Maurice tossed the book at Hakeem.

Hakeem took the book and grimly sat down at the word processor. He knew it was wrong to be doing this, but the nasty little jerk had a point. He'd get Hakeem fired and the next babysitter would play along. Hakeem would only be hurting himself.

"I'm going to be an agent for sports stars when I grow up," Maurice said, flipping channels on the TV from his chair. "Those jocks are really stupid. They need people to run their investments and stuff. I'm lots smarter than Pop. That's why I don't care that he's almost never home. I can't learn anything from him. All he knows is basketball and I hate basketball. Hakeem, what're you going to do when you finish high school? Go on welfare like your family, huh?"

"My family isn't on welfare," Hakeem snapped. "Both my parents work hard every day for what they get. I'm going to college and be a microbiologist so I can help find cures for diseases."

Maurice laughed. "That sounds really boring. My Mom is a fashion designer. That's boring, too. She's not much fun. I don't mind that she's never around 'cause she's not that much fun anyway. I like TV better than my parents. Oh! Good! A gory movie about worms that eat people."

"Maurice, your mother said you'd be working on your computer and your homework, not watching trashy TV," Hakeem said. "I don't think they'd want you to be wasting your time on that garbage."

"Hakeem, you just don't get it, do you? You're not my boss. You don't get to tell me what to do. I get to tell you what to do."

Hakeem watched in disgust as the earth throbbed with the disgusting forms of escaping monster worms who began eating up everybody in the neighborhood. The giant television screen exploded with blood and gore. "All right, look at that," Maurice said, "that's so cool. That guy who just got eaten looked like my Dad! Did you see him? Didn't he look just like superstar Dale Nash?"

Hakeem's back was turned when Maurice suddenly screamed, "Hakeem! Freeze! There's a black widow spider on your neck. Oh, no! You're doomed!"

Chapter 3

"Why do you want to do stuff like that, Maurice?" Hakeem asked sadly.

"Ha ha ha, had you going for a minute, didn't I? Didn't I? You shoulda seen yourself, Hakeem, your eyes got real big ... oh ... that was funny!" Maurice cried.

Hakeem thought 'you get a real kick out of being a jerk, don't you, kid?' But he thought too much of his job to say it out loud. "You like practical jokes, huh?" he asked.

"Yeah. I like scaring people. I like it when they shake and stuff. When I was little, I was such a big fool. My parents were gone so much I'd always think they were never coming back. I'd scream and cry. Now I don't care. I don't care if Pop plays basketball every month and never comes home. I don't care if Mom moves to Paris like she's always saying she'd like to do. I'd like to go to boarding school."

Hakeem stepped outside into the cool air and looked up at the starry night. He told himself once more that he could pile up college money fast working here. It didn't matter how obnoxious the kid was. The Nashes money was good and green. That's what mattered.

When Hakeem went back inside, the TV set was still blaring. A police show was going on with guys chasing each other and blasting away from cars. But Maurice wasn't sitting in the recliner watching.

"Maurice?" Hakeem called out. There was no answer. Hakeem felt a stab of fear. What if the kid had run away. It was Hakeem's responsibility to watch him. A rich kid like that could be kidnapped if he was wandering around outside.

"Maurice!" Hakeem shouted, running into the kitchen. It was empty. Hakeem went from room to room, his anxiety growing with the discovery of each empty room. "Maurice, where are you? Please answer me!"

Hakeem searched the upstairs. Breathlessly he yanked open closets only to find them empty. He was beginning to feel real panic. If he didn't find Maurice soon he'd have to call his parents.

Hakeem went back downstairs where the TV blared. Only now a note was pasted to the TV screen. Scrawled on the paper were these words:

Maurice is in our hands. We demand a billion dollars or he will never again be seen by human eyes.

"A *billion* dollars?" Hakeem repeated aloud. The handwriting looked like Maurice's.

Suddenly from upstairs there was the sound of chairs overturning and tables falling. It came from the rear guest room. Hakeem ran up the stairs towards the ruckus. When he charged into the darkened room he never saw the rope strung across the doorway. Hakeem plunged head first into the room, skidding across the floor.

Maurice sat on the bed laughing. "What a clumsy ox you are, Hakeem. You could never play basketball."

"You!" Hakeem yelled, lunging at the boy and grabbing him by the shoulders. He wanted to shake some sense into the brat.

But Maurice grinned into his face and shrieked, "Manhandle me one little bit and you're looking at jail time, man. When I put a mouse in old lady Jackson's sweater she tried to swat me, but I fixed her wagon. I made her life so miserable she had a nervous breakdown."

Hakeem was ready to quit. Good money or not, he didn't think he could stand another minute with this monstrous troll. Then he remembered how hard it was for a sixteen year old to earn above minimum wage. He remembered taking home all those uneaten granola bars to his own brothers and sisters. He remembered his college dreams. He slowly took his hands off of Maurice.

"That's better, you big gorilla," Maurice said.

Chapter 4

When Hakeem got home at eight, he was drained. Running around the house after Maurice wore him out emotionally and physically. But the good part was that Mrs. Nash was so pleased when she got home that she gave Hakeem a bonus of a full day's pay. "I realize how trying a bright and active boy like Maurice can be, and I really appreciate your dedication, Hakeem," she said. It was almost as if she knew what a devil her son was, and she was paying Hakeem to continue to put up with it.

"I'm home, darling," she called to Maurice.

"Who cares?" he answered.

Mrs. Nash managed a strained smile. "He has such a sense of humor for a child! Actually, he's devoted to me," she said.

"Yeah," Hakeem said, going along with the charade. Now, in his own room, Hakeem sank into the lumpy, frayed sofa and closed his eyes in exhaustion.

"Hard day, angel?" Mom asked.

"Oh, yeah, Ma. That Maurice is pretty awful," Hakeem said. He glanced at his own brothers, seven year old Jayson and eight year old Lovell. They were amusing three year old Jedra. "Ma, you got no idea what wonderful kids you have! Man, like they've got hand-me-down clothes and not many toys and they're sweet and cheerful ..."

Mom laughed. "Well, my kids aren't perfect but they're pretty lovable!"

"That Maurice, he's got state-of-the-art computers, and a wall-sized TV. He's been to Europe and Australia already, and he's a miserable little jerk!" Hakeem groaned. "If his parents buy him a shirt and he doesn't like it, he rips it to shreds and they let him!"

Mom shook her head. "That is so sad. They are cheating that boy of discipline. They must not love him."

"Oh, they brag about him and they seem to adore him," Hakeem said.

"No, honey. They probably don't love him, so they're trying to make up for that by giving him all the things he doesn't need. It's like when a husband won't give his wife a hug and gives her expensive roses.... Things can't make up for love," Mom said.

Hakeem smiled. "Pa gives you plenty of hugs, Ma."

Hakeem's father appeared in the doorway. "But he can't afford roses, sweet thing," he chuckled.

Hakeem spent two hours after dinner on his homework. He had a History and Biology quiz the next day. Then he crawled into bed and slept like a rock until dawn.

Valle Verde High School was within biking distance of Hakeem's house. He enjoyed biking down the street, past the House of the Nile where Ethiopian food was served, past the Mandarin Inn and the Dragon Garden, past the art galleries and the martial arts school.

"You look tired," Charlie Myers, Hakeem's friend said.

"I'm beat," Hakeem admitted.

"What you need is to kick back and take some time off," Charlie said.

"I wish," Hakeem groaned. "I need to save for college, and I'm making good money. Mom and Pop saved some, but if I spend it all, then what's going to happen when the younger kids in the family need money for an education?"

Brandy Taylor, a girl Hakeem had taken out a few times, came over. "Coming to the jazz concert tonight,

Hakeem? I'm playing in it."

"I'd love to, Brandy, but I'm working," Hakeem said.

Brandy's smile faded. "Oh," she said. Hakeem wondered how long it would be before Brandy got another boyfriend with him neglecting her like this. Probably not very long.

"Hey, Brandy, maybe we could do something on the weekend. I'm off then," Hakeem called to her.

"Maybe. We'll see," she said. She seemed really disappointed that he wouldn't hear her play in the concert.

Chapter 5

Hakeem arrived at the Nash house as usual and hurried up the walk. He put out Maurice's granola bars, knowing he'd refuse them as usual. But he had to at least try to carry out the parents' orders.

"Hi, Hakeem, old sport," Maurice said as he came up the walk from school. He seemed in a good mood.

"I suppose you don't want your granola bars again. You'll want candy," Hakeem said.

"No candy today," Maurice said. "I stopped and had a pepperoni pizza and I'm full. Ate at the Gourmet Inn."

"You got enough pocket money to buy pepperoni pizza?" Hakeem asked.

"It must be ten bucks a slice at that place."

Maurice shrugged. "I'm loaded." He opened his wallet and Hakeem was astonished to see at least fifty dollars in bills.

"Your parents let you carry that much money to school, Maurice?" Hakeem asked.

Maurice laughed. "Don't sweat it, old sport. Actually I've got about seventy here and ..." He was counting the money when a credit card fell out. Hakeem snatched it up before Maurice could retrieve it.

"Gimme that, you jerk!" Maurice screamed, grasping for the card.

It was a gold card bearing the name *Anita Crawford*. "That's your 6th grade teacher, isn't it?" Hakeem demanded. "How did you get her credit card?"

"I picked it up by mistake. I'm giving it back to her tomorrow," Maurice yelled. "Now give it to me!"

"Maurice, you got liar written all over your face," Hakeem said "I bet you rifled her wallet. That's where you got the cash, too!"

"It was just a joke," Maurice screeched. "She's so stupid. She leaves her purse right on her desk. So I took a little money and the credit card. I just wanted to show her how stupid it is to leave her purse like that."

"Maurice, you've already spent some of her money," Hakeem said.

"A lousy fifteen bucks? I can make that up out of my piggy bank!" Maurice said.

"Maurice, this is serious. This is stealing," Hakeem said.

"Don't you dare tell my parents," Maurice cried. "You hear me, Hakeem? If you tell on me I'll get you fired!"

"What you did was a crime," Hakeem said.

"I always take money from Mom's purse, and I don't always tell her. So what's the big deal?" Maurice asked.

"That's bad, too, but your teacher isn't family. You stole from a stranger," Hakeem said.

Maurice looked frightened. "They'll flip if you tell on me, Hakeem. They'll take away my TV, and I won't be able to go to Europe with my grandfather this summer. He's the only one who likes me. He's going to take me hiking in the Alps."

"You expect me to cover something like this up? Then it'll be on my conscience if you continue stealing and end up in prison," Hakeem said.

"Hakeem, listen. I know you're poor, so here's the deal. I can lift twenty bucks a week from Mom's purse and slip it to you. She'll never know the difference. Think about it! Twenty bucks a week extra for you! Maybe I can get even more from Dad's wallet. Sometimes when he drinks he gambles, and he forgets what he loses.

You can really cash in, Hakeem. I can get you tickets to playoffs and stuff like that, too," Maurice pleaded, his eyes wild.

Hakeem looked at the boy. He was ten years old, and he was comfortable with stealing. When he was Hakeem's age who knows what he might be willing to do.

Chapter 6

"Oh, Maurice," Hakeem groaned, "it's much worse than I thought."

"Wait here," Maurice said. He raced upstairs and returned with his mother's jewelry box, overflowing with diamonds and emeralds and rubies. They were so dazzling that they almost blinded Hakeem. "Take something for your girlfriend. Mom won't even miss it. This isn't her real good stuff, but it's good. Your girlfriend will freak if you give her something like this. If Mom does find it missing, she can just report it to the insurance company. They'll pay her money. Go on, Hakeem, take anything."

"Maurice, don't you understand,

that would be *stealing*. I'm not a thief!"

"Who'd know you took it?" Maurice demanded.

"God would know and I'd know!" Hakeem said.

Maurice took his mother's jewelry back to her bedroom. He sulked as they both waited for his mother to return from work. One last time Maurice said to Hakeem, "Tell on me and I'll make you wish you were dead!"

When Jessa Nash came home, Hakeem took a deep breath and said, "Mrs. Nash, this is really hard for me to do, but I must tell you for your son's sake. He stole some money and a credit card from his teacher's purse today."

"What?" gasped Jessa Nash, groping for the arm of a chair to sit down.

"It was a joke!" Maurice screamed. "I just wanted to teach her not to be so stupid where she left her purse."

Maurice's mother took the credit card and the cash then she called

Maurice's teacher. "Mrs. Crawford? My son has something that belongs to you. I see. You left your purse in your desk and when you came back from lunch seventy dollars and a credit card was gone. Yes, we have it. I will personally bring Maurice to school tomorrow morning. He will apologize and return your money and credit card. I am deeply, deeply sorry. And my husband and I will be making a very nice contribution to the PTA this year. Of course. Thank you." She put down the phone and glared at Maurice. "How dare you humiliate me like this? You shamed us in front of your teacher. Now she thinks we are common trash!" she cried.

"Kim Lambert stole the purse and gave it to me," Maurice screamed. "It wasn't my fault!"

"Stop lying!" Maurice's mother said coldly.

"Hakeem told me to do it," Maurice

shouted, "and he said we'd split the money!"

"Shame on you, Maurice," his mother cried. "Hakeem had the courage to do the right thing and now you're lying about him, too! Oh, I wish you'd never been born!"

Maurice stood there, a single tear poised on one eye. "I don't care!" he said.

"There will be no TV for you for a month. And probably no trip to Europe with your grandfather. If you're not very careful, young man, you'll be living in a very strict military academy instead of in this house!" Jessa Nash's voice was cold.

Hakeem was shaking from the ordeal when he left the Nash house that evening. Every time Maurice looked at him it was with a hatred so intense that it made Hakeem's blood run cold.

Hakeem walked down the driveway, knowing he'd done the right thing. He stopped once and looked back. Something inside him made him do it, but when he did, he wished he hadn't. Maurice was up in his bedroom staring out the window. The boy had written in black letters on the glass, *You will pay!*

Chapter 7

Hakeem hurried towards the bus stop. Someday, he thought, Maurice will thank me. He'll look back on this day and realize that somebody cared enough to risk a lot to turn him around. He'd obviously been stealing for a long time and getting away with it. He'd graduated to his teacher's purse after stealing at home for a long time. Maybe by middle school he'd be using his computer to rip off companies. He was bright enough for that. Maybe he'd get the chance to grow up in prison like so many kids Hakeem knew did.

Hakeem met Brandy at 9:00 that evening to go to a movie. He was glad for the chance to laugh at a funny, mindless movie and get his mind off Maurice. They shared a pizza, but Hakeem continued to worry.

"Sometimes I wish I'd never found that job with the Nashes," Hakeem said.

"The kid's getting to you, huh?" Brandy asked.

"Yeah. I dread what he'll do next. It's like a battle of wills between us. And the terrible part is, he's so clever. He's like an evil genius. But still, he's a ten year old kid and something deep down inside my soul wants to push him in the right direction," Hakeem said.

"You're a good person, Hakeem," Brandy said. "Even if you didn't come and see me play the piano like Count Basie!"

When Hakeem returned to work at 8 Tulip Lane, Maurice seemed almost nice. He dutifully ate his granola bars and then settled down to do his homework. Hakeem was not a fool. He knew Maurice was up to something. He kept waiting for the other shoe to drop.

"You might as well do your homework, too, Hakeem," Maurice said, "because I'll be busy with my history homework."

"Okay," Hakeem said. "I have a lot to do in biology."

"Is that Ms. Toalingo a good teacher?" Maurice asked.

"How'd you know my biology teacher's name, Maurice?" Hakeem asked.

"Oh, you left your papers laying there the other day and I saw it. Is she from India?" Maurice asked.

"Yeah. She's very good, too," Hakeem said.

It turned out to be the best afternoon Hakeem ever spent at the Nash house. He got all his homework done. Maurice was perfect. Hakeem dared to hope that maybe the boy had decided to get his act together.

Hakeem actually felt rested when he went home that evening. He could curl up with a good book and even spend some time with his friends on the telephone.

In the morning Hakeem arrived early to his honors' biology class. He turned in his homework and Ms. Toalingo said, "Just a moment, Hakeem." She reached in her desk drawer and pulled out a letter written by a computer. She handed it to Hakeem, and he read it with shock.

Dearest one. I have loved you for a long time. I had to tell you of my love or my heart would burst. Be mine or I will die. Yours forever, Hakeem Kemp.

Ms. Toalingo was smiling but Hakeem's face was on fire. "Some of your friends must be practical jokers, Hakeem," she said.

"I'm really embarrassed," Hakeem said.

"Don't be. I knew immediately it wasn't from you. You are far too sensible a boy to fall in love with a teacher and especially one my age," Ms. Toalingo said.

"I'm afraid the author of this letter is a vengeful ten year old boy who wants to make trouble for me!" Hakeem said.

"Well, I'd burn the silly letter, Hakeem, and send that child to bed without his dessert!" the teacher laughed.

But Hakeem was seething. That wicked little troll was reaching into his personal life to wreak havoc!

Chapter 8

When Hakeem saw Maurice that afternoon he told him about the letter.

Maurice shrugged, "Man, that must've really made you feel crummy, Hakeem," he said.

"Did you give that letter to my teacher, Maurice?" Hakeem said.

"Me? I'm just a little kid. How would I figure out how to do that?" Maurice said. "Anyway, I bet your teacher thinks you're a big jerk now, huh?"

"No, she knows me well enough to realize I didn't send the letter. Listen, Maurice, do something like that again and you're in major trouble, understand?" Hakeem said.

"You can't prove I did it," Maurice said, his eyes glowing with hatred. "I'll get you, Hakeem. You got my parents on your side now, but I've just begun to fight."

At school the next day, Hakeem saw Brandy across the campus. "Hey, Brandy, I'm free this weekend and ..." he called to her.

"Oh, Hakeem, I'm sorry but I'm not. My church group is going on a special camping trip. We'll be gone until late Sunday night," Brandy said.

Hakeem felt like he'd been slapped in the face. He knew he shouldn't feel that way. Brandy was active at church. He shouldn't expect her to drop everything and go out with him when he had a free day. He suspected that maybe Brandy had another boyfriend. Maybe she'd gotten tired of him being so busy.

Hakeem was thinking so hard about Brandy that he didn't even hear when

Ms. Lansing called on him in English. "Stop daydreaming, Hakeem," Ms. Lansing snapped.

Just before Hakeem left English class, someone from the office came in with a note for him. He read it and all the feeling drained from his legs. *Call home. Dad has been in an accident. Mom.*

Hakeem stumbled to the telephone and dialed with numb fingers. When his mother answered he said, "Mom, I got your note. How's Dad? What happened?"

"What note?" Hakeem's mother said. "Dad is right here making a lamp. What are you talking about?"

"Mom ... somebody called the school saying they were you and that Dad was in an accident," Hakeem cried.

"Oh, angel, what monster would play such a trick!" Mom gasped.

Hakeem put down the phone, shaking now with rage. The little fiend must have called the school and left the false message to torment Hakeem!

Hakeem waited that afternoon as Maurice came up the walk whistling. Hakeem grabbed his arm and yanked him inside. "Don't you ever, ever call my school and scare me like that again, Maurice. You hear me?" Hakeem shouted in the boy's face.

"I didn't do anything," Maurice said. "And you better let go of me. If you leave a mark on my arm I'll say you beat me up. Then you'll go to jail. Ha ha ha ha."

Hakeem looked at the boy. He hated him. He had never hated another human being before in his life, but the child was evil. There was no other way to put it. "I'm warning you, Maurice, one more dirty trick and I'll talk your parents into sending you to the meanest military school on earth. I can do it, too. They respect me now."

Maurice stared right into Hakeem's eyes, "I don't care. Mom and Dad don't like me. They never want to be with me. Only my grandfather likes me, and now you messed that up. I won't get to go to the Alps this summer with him." The boy's eyes sparkled with tears of rage.

"Maurice, if you stop this garbage maybe your parents will change their mind and let you go to the Alps with your grandfather," Hakeem said.

"Nah. You're just saying that to get me off your back. But it won't work. You will pay, Hakeem. You will pay," the boy chanted.

Chapter 9

Hakeem took off his coat and put it in the closet. He planned to do his history report today and heaven help that brat if he bothered him.

When Hakeem walked into the living room he didn't see Maurice. "Maurice! Look, I'm not chasing all over looking for you."

Maurice's voice came from upstairs. "I'm in the bedroom."

Hakeem went up the stairs. "I want you down here where I can make sure you're doing your homework." At that, Hakeem heard Maurice running up the stairs to the attic. "Maurice! Your parents don't want you messing in the attic!"

Hakeem went up the attic stairs himself. He opened the door and peered in. It was too dark to see much. "Come out of there, Maurice," he yelled. "I'm getting sick of your stupid little games!"

Hakeem moved slowly into the attic, searching for Maurice, unaware that the boy had slipped out behind him. Suddenly the attic door slammed shut behind Hakeem.

Hakeem raced to the door but it was locked from the outside.

"Now you're trapped, you slime bug," Maurice screeched. "I can do anything I want. I'm roasting marshmallows and making popcorn and turning on the television so loud the walls will shake! Mom won't be home for hours. I'm the boss!"

"Maurice, let me out of here," Hakeem yelled.

"I'm gonna burn your books in the fireplace," Maurice said. "I'm gonna burn all your homework so you get in trouble at school."

The boy ran down the steps roaring with laughter.

Hakeem found one small window in the attic. It was stuck shut. Maybe if he pushed hard enough he could get it open, crawl out onto the porch roof, and climb down on the balcony.

"That little monster," Hakeem fumed as he tried to open the window. Finally it yielded. He inched out onto the roof but he was three stories up and a fall could prove fatal. As Hakeem moved gingerly over the roof, he smelled smoke.

Maurice was probably burning his books like he'd threatened! Or maybe he'd started a fire in the kitchen making popcorn. Whatever it was, there seemed to be a lot of smoke. What if he set the whole house on fire?

Hakeem gripped the balcony with his fingertips. Once he almost lost his footing, but he caught himself. With maddeningly slow moves, he made it down the side of the house, dropping at last to the earth below. Then Hakeem looked up to see smoke pouring from several windows.

"Oh, my God!" Hakeem gasped, "He's set the house on fire!" Hakeem screamed to a neighbor across the street, "Call the fire department!" The woman nodded and ran back inside her house.

"Maurice!" Hakeem yelled. "Get out of there!" Hakeem figured the boy had run from the house in terror the minute he saw the fire getting out of control, but maybe not. Maybe he was cowering somewhere inside the house. "Maurice!" Hakeem yelled. "Where are you?"

Hakeem stepped back to see Maurice at the window of his bedroom on the second floor. He'd run upstairs to the false security of his bedroom when the kitchen was in flames. The bright kid had done a stupid, typically childish thing.

"Help me!" Maurice screamed. "I'm gonna burn up!"

Hakeem drenched himself with the garden hose and raced back inside the house, plunging into the dense rolling smoke, a wet rag over his face. He had to get Maurice out of there. He had to. The fire department would get there too late at the rate the old house was going up in flames.

Chapter 10

Hakeem crawled on the floor to Maurice's bedroom.

"Maurice, come to me!" he screamed.

The smoke was thicker, darker, and choking now. Hakeem thought that maybe he would die here. He'd made a fateful decision, and he might pay for it with his life.

Hakeem got to the bedroom window and found the boy sobbing. "We're gonna die. We're gonna burn up," he sobbed. Hakeem picked him up in his arms and turned, but the fire blocked the route he'd come by. The stairs he'd just climbed were fiery now.

Hakeem carried Maurice to the window and threw a chair through the glass, smashing it. He battered the jagged shards away and crawled out onto the roof.

"That tree branch," Hakeem gasped, "we can climb to that. Maurice, hang onto my back. Put your arms around my neck and don't let go!"

Maurice's arms almost strangled Hakeem as he crawled onto the branch of an oak tree near the window. Hakeem worked his way down the tree as the uppermost branches of the tree itself burst into flames.

As the fire engines wailed, Hakeem dropped to the ground with Maruice, both of them unhurt except for some bruises and smoke inhalation. Hakeem lay on the ground breathing hard, staring at the inferno that was claiming the old mansion.

Maurice's mother appeared soon after the firemen. Maurice's father was back east with his basketball team. Mrs.

Nash stared at the house, tears running down her face. "All my beautiful things," she wailed. "There were so many things that cannot be replaced."

"I'm sorry, Mom," Maurice said. "I was making popcorn. It got real hot and started burning. I didn't know what to do."

"Shut up!" the woman cried. "You wicked, wicked boy. After all we've given you, how could you do this to us? Well, it'll be military school for you. I've had it. You've messed up my life for the last time, Maurice Nash!"

Hakeem watched with growing disgust and sadness. He had the phone number of Maurice's grandfather in case of emergencies. He slipped away and called the man. In about ten minutes a car pulled up with two elderly people in it. The man had white hair that stood out dramatically against his dark skin. The woman was tiny and pretty with light brown skin. They rushed to the forlorn figure of the little boy and gathered him up.

"I've had it, Mother," Mrs. Nash said. "I almost hate him."

"It's all right, Jessa," the older woman said gently. "He can stay with us for a while, and then we'll see ..."

Hakeem was walking away from the fire scene when the boy yelled at him. "Hakeem!" He turned and walked over. "Yeah, Maurice?"

"You saved me," Maurice said.

"Yeah," Hakeem admitted.

"How come?" the boy asked.

Hakeem smiled a little and wiped a smudge of ash off the boy's nose. "Hang in there, kid," he said.

When Hakeem got home the phone was ringing. "I heard about the fire," Brandy said. "Everybody is saying you're a hero, Hakeem."

"Nah. I just did what I had to," Hakeem said.

"You're a good person, Hakeem,"

Brandy said. "And ... uh, did I ever tell you that I loved you?"

"I don't think you ever did," Hakeem said softly, his heart pounding.

"Well, I do," she said.

The smell of smoke faded from Hakeem's nostrils. From somewhere he smelled roses, and he could swear somebody, somewhere, was playing the sweetest music this side of heaven.

About a month after the fire, Hakeem got a phone call from Maurice's grandfather. "Having a barbecue Sunday. Wife and I want you to come over, Hakeem. Please, feel free to bring a friend."

Hakeem and Brandy caught a bus to a neighborhood of ranch-style houses Sunday afternoon. Lately, Hakeem didn't have the money to take Brandy many places. She didn't seem to mind, but he did. He couldn't do much on his minimum wage job at the taco stand.

Hakeem spotted Maurice in the backyard of the house. He looked different. It was puzzling. He wasn't taller or fatter or dressed differently. He just looked oddly changed.

"Hi, Hakeem," the boy said with a warm grin.

"Hi, Maurice. Good to see you," Hakeem said.

Hakeem and Brandy tried the ribs. They were something special. "These are the best," Hakeem told Maurice's grandfather.

"I cooked for a living before I retired," the man said. "Those were the good times ... house full of kids ... then me and my wife retired. But, well, ... it got lonely around here." Tears sparkled in his eyes. His wife grasped his arm. She was crying, too. "Thanks to you, Hakeem, we got our precious grandson to love. You saved him for us." With that the man gave Hakeem a check.

Hakeem gasped at the amount. It was enough for college and then some! Maurice's grandmother quickly patted his hand and said, "It's nothing."

Maurice stood there grinning. Hakeem knew what it was that changed him so. He was loved now, and it showed.